Agent Rookie's Secret Mission

PICK YOUR PATH 8

Agent Rookie's Secret Mission

PICK YOUR PATH 8

by Tracey West

Grosset & Dunlap
An Imprint of Penguin Group (USA) Inc.

GROSSET & DUNLAP
Published by the Penguin Group
Penguin Group (USA) Inc., 375 Hudson Street,
New York, New York 10014, USA
Penguin Group (Canada), 90 Eglinton Avenue East, Suite 700,
Toronto, Ontario M4P 2Y3, Canada
(a division of Pearson Penguin Canada Inc.)
Penguin Books Ltd, 80 Strand, London WC2R 0RL, England
Penguin Ireland, 25 St Stephen's Green, Dublin 2, Ireland
(a division of Penguin Books Ltd)
Penguin Group (Australia), 707 Collins Street,
Melbourne, Victoria 3008, Australia
(a division of Pearson Australia Group Pty Ltd)
Penguin Books India Pvt Ltd, 11 Community Centre,
Panchsheel Park, New Delhi—110 017, India
Penguin Group (NZ), 67 Apollo Drive, Rosedale, Auckland 0632, New Zealand
(a division of Pearson New Zealand Ltd)
Penguin Books, Rosebank Office Park, 181 Jan Smuts Avenue,
Parktown North 2193, South Africa
Penguin China, B7 Jaiming Center, 27 East Third Ring Road North,
Chaoyang District, Beijing 100020, China

Penguin Books Ltd, Registered Offices:
80 Strand, London WC2R 0RL, England

Printed in the U.S.A.

ISBN 978-0-448-46273-8 10 9 8 7 6 5 4 3 2 1

“Perfect!” you say, smoothing out the snow on top of the pirate’s hat. “Now all I have to do is get his beard just right.”

You’re in the Snow Forts making a sculpture of Captain Rockhopper out of snow. It’s life-size, and you think it’s your best snow creation yet. You’ve been working on it for hours and can’t wait to show your friends. Taking a step back, you admire what you’ve done so far.

Bonk! Bonk! Bonk! Bonk! A barrage of snowballs appears out of nowhere, slamming into your sculpture. You watch in disbelief as they knock off Captain Rockhopper’s pirate hat, turning it into a spray of snow.

You turn in the direction of the snowballs, shaking your head.

“I don’t mind a good snowball fight, but you seem to have knocked over my sculpture,” you say politely.

But the snowball thrower isn’t listening. The excited green penguin keeps chucking snowballs at your Captain Rockhopper. He’s wearing red sunglasses and a red-and-white propeller beanie.

“I’ve got you, Herbert!” he cries, tackling

the snow sculpture. It crumbles, covering the green penguin with snow.

"What's going on?" you wonder, confused, when a red penguin calmly approaches you. He's wearing a black suit and a crisp white shirt, and a cool pair of black wraparound shades covers his eyes.

"Rookie, I told you that's not Herbert," he tells the green penguin.

"But he's big and white and—oh," Rookie replies, his voice falling. You can tell that he's realized he just made a big mistake. He stands up, sheepishly brushing the snow off him. Then he turns to you.

"Sorry," he says, "but your snow sculpture sure looked like Herbert from a distance."

"Herbert?" you ask.

The red penguin is shaking his head. "You've got a lot of enthusiasm, Rookie, but you need to think before you act. Try counting to ten next time. For now, clean up this penguin's sculpture and then report to HQ right away. I've got some gear that needs polishing."

"Yes, sir," Rookie agrees with a sigh.

The red penguin turns and walks away,

and you see that he's got a jet pack strapped to his back. Suddenly, you realize who these two penguins are.

"Hey, you're Rookie, from the EPF, and that was Jet Pack Guy!" you say excitedly. "I've read a lot about you. Wow, it's really cool to meet you in person. I'm a member of the Elite Penguin Force, too, you know, but I'm not famous like you guys."

"Jet Pack Guy is the real superstar," Rookie says a little sadly. "I'm always messing things up."

You seem to remember reading that Rookie is responsible for letting the bots loose in *System Defender*, so he might have a point.

"Maybe, but you have some pretty cool adventures," you point out. "I've read all about them in *The Club Penguin Times*. You're the Communications Lead, right?"

Rookie brightens up. "That's me. Rookie's my name, communications is my game!"

"Well, that's an important job," you say.

"I know," Rookie says, nodding his head. "It's just—I wish that once, just once, I could impress Jet Pack Guy! He's so smooth! He's so cool! But I'm pretty sure that I annoy him sometimes."

"I bet there's a way you can impress him,"

ay. "Like, maybe you could solve a big case he EPF or something."

"Maybe I could!" he says, his voice rising with excitement. "That would be super! You know, I've always wanted to find a real golden puffle. If I did that, Jet Pack Guy would *have* to be impressed."

"I thought the golden puffle was just a play," you say, confused.

"It *is* a play," Rookie replies. "But there are lots of rumors on the island that it's based on a real puffle that's gold. Some penguins say they've seen it. Wouldn't it be great if the rumors were true and we're the ones who find it?"

"We?" you ask. "You mean, you and me?"

"Sure!" Rookie says. "If I'm going to go searching for the golden puffle, I'll need some help. Can I count on you?"

"You bet!" you reply, and now you're the one who's excited. Searching for the golden puffle sounds like an exciting mission. "So, what do we do?"

"I think we should check on the latest rumors," Rookie says. "And the best place to hear rumors on Club Penguin is in the Town Center."

"Then let's go!" you say.

You and Rookie waddle into the Town Center. Dozens of penguins are gathered on the street in front of the Night Club. Just like Rookie said, the rumors are flying fast.

"I heard Gary the Gadget Guy is a time traveler," you hear a green penguin say.

A yellow penguin is spreading another rumor. "I heard there's a ghost at the top of the Lighthouse."

"I heard that a penguin slid down the Bunny Hill and was never seen again," a purple penguin is saying.

Rookie looks at you and shakes his head. Nothing! Then a red penguin gets your attention.

"I heard a real golden puffle was seen in the Forest," he tells his friend.

Rookie rushes up to the red penguin. "A gold puffle? In the Forest?"

The red penguin nods. "Yeah. My friend's brother's cousin saw it."

Rookie looks at you. "Now we know where to start!"

"I don't know," you say. "These rumors are

kind of ridiculous. This all started with the play at the Stage, right? Maybe that would be a better place to start."

Rookie looks thoughtful. "Hmm. You may have a point there."

If you and Rookie go to the Stage, go to page 41.

If you and Rookie go to the Forest, go to page 53.

CONTINUED FROM PAGE 58.

"Full speed ahead!" Rookie cries, and he sends the Aqua Grabber zooming forward. Once you reach the air vent, a huge air bubble envelops you.

Klepto is catching up, but Rookie is one determined penguin. He steers up to the surface, leaving Klepto in his wake. Once you break through the water, Rookie can retract the claw. He exits the Aqua Grabber, triumphantly waving the ruby.

"We did it! We rescued the missing ruby!"

You climb out and congratulate him. "Great job, Rookie!"

"Yes. Nice work, Rookie."

You and Rookie turn to see Jet Pack Guy standing there.

"Jet Pack Guy! What are you doing here?" Rookie asks.

"G put me on the case of the missing ruby, and I saw the crab tracks and figured that Klepto was our culprit," Jet Pack Guy says. "But I see you beat me to it. Good job."

Jet Pack Guy high-fives Rookie.

"Woo-hoo!" Rookie cheers. "Did you see that? Jet Pack Guy just high-fived me. Me! Rookie! This guy right here!"

"Looks like your wish came true," you say.

Rookie grins. "I couldn't have done it without you. Thanks!"

THE END

CONTINUED FROM PAGE 80.

“Pizza is the heart and soul of Club Penguin!” Rookie argues. “Penguins love to eat it, they love to make it, and they love to serve it. I’m sure that Protobot is planning on stealing all the pizza. We’ve got to hurry!”

Rookie rushes off before you can say anything, and you hurry to keep up with him. When you arrive at the Pizza Parlor, things look normal. Penguins are seated at the small, round tables, eating slices of pizza in the flickering candlelight. Servers in aprons are busily scurrying around the tables, and a cashier is ringing up orders on the cash register.

“Everything looks good,” you say.

“That’s because Protobot hasn’t struck yet!” Rookie says. He clears his throat. “Excuse me, everybody! Sorry to disturb you, but we’re in the middle of an EPF emergency here. This Pizza Parlor is closed!”

There’s a groan from the penguins as they reluctantly leave their tables. Rookie runs into the kitchen and bursts back through the door balancing a huge stack of pizzas.

"Whoa!" you cry. "What's all that for?"

"It's evidence!" Rookie says. "Come on, let's get these to HQ, stat."

"Um, maybe we should transport there," you say as the tall stack of pizza boxes dangerously sways back and forth. "You know, with our spy phones."

"Good idea," Rookie agrees. "My phone's right in my pocket."

Rookie takes one flipper out from under the pile of boxes, and they start to sway even more wildly.

"I got it!" you say quickly, holding up your spy phone, and you breathe a sigh of relief when Rookie puts his flipper back under the pile.

You call up HQ on your phone and press a button. Instantly, you and Rookie are transported from the Pizza Parlor into EPF Headquarters.

You arrive in the middle of an incredible scene. On one side of you are three penguins: Jet Pack Guy, Dot, and G, the EPF Agent who is also known as Gary the Gadget Guy. On the other side of you is a giant robot. His body is made from an old ticket booth and a wheeled mine cart. His arms are made from other spare parts, and his metal head and yellow, glowing eyes resemble an evil penguin.

"Protobot!" Rookie yells.

"I am Protobot. Surrender or be destroyed," the robot says in a monotone voice. Then he charges forward.

"Ahhhh!"

Startled, Rookie stumbles, and the tower of pizza boxes comes crashing down. Box lids fly open, and the floor is quickly covered with slippery cheese and tomato sauce.

Protobot wheels right over the pizza—and slips. The giant villain topples over, and Jet Pack Guy and Dot spring into action, quickly opening up Protobot's control panel and shutting him down.

G walks up to you and Rookie. "Excellent work, Rookie," G praises your new friend. "Your timing was perfect. Protobot is defeated once more, and I know just the way to celebrate."

"How?" you ask.

G grins. "With a pizza party, of course!"

THE END

CONTINUED FROM PAGE 28.

The catapult seems a little scary to you, so you decide to go with the Jet Pack for Two, even though it's experimental.

"Good choice!" Rookie says. "We can just zip up to the top of the tree and grab the golden puffle. Jet Pack Guy will have to be impressed."

The two of you transport back to the tree.

"All righty," Rookie says brightly. "Let's strap in!"

You stand next to Rookie, and each of you pulls a set of straps over your shoulders, fastening them tightly. Rookie touches the big red button on the controls.

"Ready for liftoff?" he asks.

"As ready as I'll ever be," you reply.

"One . . . two . . . three . . . let's go!" Rookie shouts.

The motor of the Jet Pack for Two roars to life. Your stomach lurches as it lifts you and Rookie off the ground and up, up, up into the air.

"Whee! It works!" Rookie cheers.

"We've got to get closer to the tree," you point out.

"I think we can steer by leaning our bodies, like this," Rookie says.

He leans forward and to the right, and you do the same. You soar right up to the top of the tree, closer and closer to the bright flash of gold.

"It's the golden puffle!" Rookie cries.

But when you get closer, you see it's just some leftover tinsel from a holiday tree.

"Rats!" Rookie says. "But I'm not giving up. Let's fly around. Maybe we can spot the golden puffle from up here."

He leans to the right, and you do the same—but the Jet Pack for Two swerves to the left.

Put-put-put-put-put. The motor starts making strange noises. The Jet Pack for Two spins and whirls wildly in the air. It's out of control!

"We're going to crash!" you yell as you begin to plummet to the Forest floor. You close your eyes, bracing for the worst, and then . . .

Splash! You land in the deep, cold water of a creek.

As the shock from your fall registers, you realize that you and Rookie are quickly sinking

underwater. The weight of the heavy Jet Pack for Two is dragging you under.

"We've got to take off the jet pack!" Rookie yells, and you quickly unhook your straps. You're free and able to paddle and keep your head above water, but Rookie is still sinking.

"The buckle on the straps is jammed!" he says, trying to get it open. "I can't get it off."

You think fast. Your old EPF phone has special tools built in. You flip it open and choose a slim screwdriver. Then you quickly use the tool to undo the buckle. It isn't easy because Rookie is splashing a lot as he struggles to stay above water.

Then . . . *pop!* The buckle opens.

"Rookie, slide out!" you yell.

Rookie slips free of the jet pack. He's exhausted, so you half pull him as he paddles back to shore. The two of you climb onto the snowy bank and flop down on your backs.

"Thank you!" Rookie says. "You're a great agent. Jet Pack Guy would be proud of you." He sighs. "I can't believe how bad I messed up with that Jet Pack for Two! We didn't even see the golden puffle. I'm a failure!"

Rookie is feeling really down, so you try to cheer him up. "No, you're not! You're great! Let's get up and get back to town and find some other way to impress Jet Pack Guy."

Rookie jumps up. He's got his confidence back. "You're right!" he says, and then he looks at the creek. "But I'm not sure where we are. Should we head upstream or downstream?"

If you and Rookie swim upstream, go to page 22.

If you and Rookie swim downstream, go to page 32.

CONTINUED FROM PAGE 46.

"You just need more confidence," you tell Rookie. "This is your perfect chance to impress Jet Pack Guy."

"Then let's do it!" Rookie cries.

He darts down the hall back to the EPF Control Room and activates the *System Defender* program. He stares at the screen for a moment.

"I'm not sure what to do," he admits. "Protobot has already reached the mainframe. Which cannons should I use?"

"Um, try some red ones," you say.

"Okay," Rookie says. He presses some buttons.

Boom! Boom! Boom! Boom! Boom!

"All right!" you cheer.

But then you hear the sound of whirring wheels, and Protobot rolls into the Control Room. He's dented a little bit, but not damaged.

"The red cannons weren't strong enough!" Rookie wails. He starts frantically pressing buttons, but it's too late.

"New directive activated. Take over the

EPF," Protobot says, his yellow eyes flashing.

Rookie bravely runs in front of the robot. "You've got to get past me first, you bucket of bolts!"

"Victory is mine," Protobot says. He shoots a net out of his body, instantly trapping you and Rookie.

"I win," Protobot says. "The EPF is now under my control."

Rookie struggles to get through the net. "I can't break it!" he yells.

"I'm sorry," you say. "I guess we should have tried to free G and the others."

THE END

CONTINUED FROM PAGE 19.

You and Rookie decide to head upstream. The bank of the creek is steep and narrow, so you jump in and swim. The water is cold, but you can move much faster this way.

You both swim a little bit farther and then waddle out of the freezing water. You climb up the bank to the top of a rocky ridge. Shading your eyes from the sun, you look across the creek and see something gleaming in the sunlight.

"Rookie, look!" you say.

There's definitely something gold and round on the other side of the creek, but it's hard to see with the sun in your eyes. Then it hops away, into the Forest.

"Was that the golden puffle?" Rookie asks.

You shake your head. "Maybe. But we'll never know for sure."

THE END

CONTINUED FROM PAGE 58.

"The one by the rock is closest," Rookie says.

He quickly steers left and then hovers over the vent. A big bubble shoots up, enveloping the Aqua Grabber. Then the bubble lifts the craft up.

"I think we're getting away!" you say, looking down at Klepto.

But neither you nor Rookie is looking up—where a large rock overhang is blocking your path to the surface.

Bam! The Aqua Grabber bangs into the rock. You hold on tight as the craft shakes violently.

"Uh-oh," Rookie says.

The claw holding the ruby opens up, sending the ruby sinking into the depths below. Klepto skitters right up to it and grabs it with his own claws.

"We've got to follow him!" you yell.

Rookie steers the Aqua Grabber back down, but Klepto is going deep into the water.

The water is darker, and it's hard to follow Klepto, but Rookie stays on him.

Then . . . *whoosh!* The Aqua Grabber starts to quickly float to the surface.

"Rats! We're out of air!" Rookie says.

Seconds later, you're bobbing on top of the water. To your surprise, Jet Pack Guy is standing on the edge of the Iceberg wearing scuba gear.

"G and I traced the missing ruby to Klepto's lair," he says. "Did you find it?"

"We found it!" Rookie says proudly. "And then we . . . um . . . lost it."

Jet Pack Guy shakes his head. "I'll take it from here," he says matter-of-factly. Then he dives into the water.

"Oh well," Rookie says. "Guess I'm not going to impress Jet Pack Guy today!"

THE END

CONTINUED FROM PAGE 54.

"Where should we look first?" Rookie wonders.

"Well, maybe the trees," you suggest. "If the golden puffle really can fly, it might be getting away."

Rookie springs to attention. "Why didn't I think of that? Let's hurry!"

He races ahead of you, and you have to hurry to keep up. Soon you're in the middle of the Forest, weaving your way between the trees.

"It's kind of hard to see the sky from here," you point out.

"No problem!" Rookie says, skidding to a stop. He whips out two pairs of binoculars and hands one to you. "Let's keep our eyes on the skies!"

You both continue walking, a little more slowly this time, with your eyes peeled on the treetops. For a long time you see nothing but blue sky, clouds, and green branches. Then, suddenly . . .

"What's that?" you ask. Something shiny is glinting in the very top of one of the trees.

Rookie aims his binoculars at it. "Hmm. I can't quite make it out. But it *is* shiny. Maybe it's the golden puffle! Wouldn't that be great? Jet Pack Guy will be so impressed with me!"

"There's only one way to find out for sure," you say. "We've got to get to the top of that tree. It's too bad we can't fly."

"Let's transport to HQ. G might have something that can help us," Rookie says. He starts typing into his spy phone. "Let me just type in our coordinates, so we can come back to the same spot."

When Rookie is done, you use your spy phone to instantly transport to EPF Headquarters. The main Control Room is bustling with Agents from all over the island. Rookie leads you right to the door of G's lab and uses a security card to let you both in.

"G? Are you here?" Rookie asks, but there's no answer.

"G is Gary the Gadget Guy, right?" you ask.

Rookie nods. "Gary is famous for inventing some of the coolest things on Club Penguin, like the Pizzatron 3000," he says. "But EPF Agents know him as G, the EPF Agent who

makes cool gadgets for us."

You look around the lab. Strange gadgets and inventions of all kinds fill the shelves. The main desk is covered with coffee-stained plans for G's new creations. A few items are covered with sheets and signs labeled DON'T TOUCH! INVENTION IN PROGRESS!

"I guess we should wait until G gets back," you say.

"But this is urgent!" Rookie says. "If there's a golden puffle in that tree, we have to get back to it right away. G won't mind if we borrow something. Let's look around."

You and Rookie split up and start examining the inventions on the shelves.

"What are we looking for exactly?" you ask.

"Something that can get us to the top of that tree," Rookie replies. "Like, a balloon, or a super ladder, or . . ."

"A Jet Pack for Two?" you ask.

"That would be great, but there's no such thing as a Jet Pack for Two," Rookie says.

"But there's one right here." You've found an extra-wide jet pack with two sets of straps. It's labeled EXPERIMENTAL.

"Perfect!" Rookie says.

"Maybe it's not safe," you say, pointing to the label.

"Oh, don't worry about that," Rookie says, waving his flipper.

You're a little afraid of the jet pack, so you look around some more. Then you find a device called a Penguin Catapult. You read the diagram on the side. It looks like a penguin sits in a basket at the end of the lever. The lever gets pulled back and then . . . *whoosh!* The penguin goes flying through the air.

"How about this?" you ask Rookie.

If you and Rookie borrow the Jet Pack for Two, go to page 16.

If you and Rookie borrow the Penguin Catapult, go to page 48.

CONTINUED FROM PAGE 72.

You pick up the apple and throw it as hard as you can at Protobot. A door on the robot's chest opens up, and he catches the apple.

"Uh-oh," Rookie says.

"What's wrong?" you ask.

"Protobot can absorb items he encounters and transform them into weapons," he tells you. "We may be in trouble."

"It was just an apple," you say. "What could he do with an apple?"

Protobot's eyes glow, his body shakes, and seconds later . . . *wham!* A wave of sticky applesauce shoots from his arm, slamming into you and Rookie. The blast sends you both sliding across the floor.

"You cannot defeat me," Protobot says, and then he rolls down the hall toward the EPF mainframe.

"Stop Protobot!" Jet Pack Guy yells from the cage.

You and Rookie get to your feet and try to run to Protobot—but you slip in the applesauce again. By the time you get up, Protobot is

rolling away from the mainframe.

"Mainframe breached. Location found. Mission complete," the robot says, and then he crashes through a wall, escaping.

"Hurry!" Jet Pack Guy yells.

You get back on your feet once more and slowly and carefully make your way to the cage. You reach out to open the door, but G stops you.

"Don't! You'll be electrified," G says. He nods to Rookie. "Pull that red lever on the far wall. That should negate the cage's electric charge."

"Sure thing, boss," Rookie says and swiftly obeys. The cage stops producing an electric charge, and Jet Pack Guy jimmies the lock, freeing himself as well as Dot and G.

"Thanks," he says, nodding to you and Rookie. Then he turns to G. "I'm on this one. Don't worry, I'll stop him."

"There is no need for that," says G, a blue penguin wearing round eyeglasses and a white lab coat.

"What do you mean?" Jet Pack Guy asks. "Protobot is going to steal all of the island's coins if we don't catch him!"

"But he will not find it," G explains. "The location of the coins is top secret—so secret that it is not even stored in the mainframe. The location that I programmed into the mainframe is just a decoy."

"That's awesome!" Rookie cheers. "So where is Protobot headed?"

"To a remote cave deep in the mountains," G says, "where he will find sacks and sacks of . . . seashells."

Rookie wipes off some applesauce from his front. "I wish I could see his face when that happens," he says. "You know what I would say?"

"What?" you ask.

Rookie grins. "How do you like *those* apples, Protobot?"

THE END

CONTINUED FROM PAGE 19.

You and Rookie decide to head downstream. The Jet Pack for Two is floating on top of the creek, so you jump in the water and ride it like a raft down the creek. After a few minutes, the surrounding trees begin to look familiar.

Soon you reach the Cove and climb out. Then you and Rookie transport back to HQ.

This time, you find G, a blue penguin wearing round glasses and a white lab coat, waiting for you. "I see you've been testing my Jet Pack for Two," G says.

"Sorry, G," Rookie says. "We crashed it."

"No need to apologize," G said. "I've been looking for an Agent to test this out. Excellent job!"

Rookie turns to you and grins. "All right! G is impressed. Now I know that I'll impress Jet Pack Guy one day."

THE END

CONTINUED FROM PAGE 44.

On the way to the Beach, you and Rookie waddle past the Dock. Blue waves lap against the snowy shore, and the Hydro-Hopper bobs on the water, waiting for a penguin looking to ride the waves.

Rookie stops.

"Let's look here," he suggests. "Where there's water, there are crabs."

"Good idea," you agree, and you and Rookie comb the snow for crab tracks. But the snow is smooth and clean. There's no sign of tracks—or the ruby.

"Nothing here," Rookie says. "Let's move on to the Beach."

Then a slight breeze kicks up, and a piece of paper flutters past Rookie's beak.

"A clue!" Rookie cries, and he goes running after it.

You think it's probably a stray piece of litter, but you know by now that you can't stop Rookie once he gets an idea in his head. He chases the paper across the snowy meadow until he's able to jump up and catch it.

"Got it!" he cries, somersaulting in the snow as he lands. He reads it to himself and then waves you over. "Get a load of this!"

You quickly waddle to his side and read the paper.

IT'S ALL HAPPENING AT CPT 10:00 AT THE PLACE WHERE MUSIC RULES.

"This is clearly a message from Herbert P. Bear," he says.

"You mentioned Herbert before," you say. "What's his deal again?"

"He's a total villain," Rookie tells you. "Ever since he came to Club Penguin, he's been cooking up evil plots. He's caused earthquakes and avalanches, and once he almost sank the island!"

"Oh, yeah, I remember reading about him," you say. "Do you really think this is a message from him? It kind of looks like a flyer for a music concert."

Rookie checks his watch. "I've seen Herbert's messages before, and this one has his paws all over it," he says firmly. "We can look for the ruby later. Right now, we need to stop Herbert. It's almost ten o'clock. We just need to decipher the message. Where is a place where music rules?"

You're thoughtful. "Well, the Night Club, of course. But there's also a music stage at the Lighthouse. I saw a band play there once."

If you go to the Night Club, go to page 47.

If you go to the Lighthouse, go to page 67.

CONTINUED FROM PAGE 77.

Protobot rolls past your hiding place.

"Rookie, try that button!" you urge. "We've got to stop him!"

"Right!" Rookie agrees. He presses a button on the control panel, and the room becomes dark.

"What happened?" you ask.

"I don't know," Rookie replies anxiously. "I think I pressed the wrong button. Instead of locking the control room, I turned out the lights!"

"Try another button!" you suggest.

"I can't see!" Rookie wails.

You hear him trying a bunch of different buttons. An alarm sounds. The fire sprinklers go off, dousing you with water. Finally, the lights go back on.

"Got it!" Rookie says. He climbs out from under the table, and you follow him. "You're trapped, Protobot!"

But Protobot is nowhere in sight. He's escaped!

The sounds of cannons stop, and Jet Pack Guy, Dot, and G come running toward you.

"Where is he?" Jet Pack Guy asks.

“He got away,” Rookie replies.

Jet Pack Guy shakes his head. “Typical. Dot, let’s go see if we can track that bot.”

Jet Pack Guy and Dot leave. Rookie sadly hangs his head. “Sorry, G.”

“No need to be sorry,” G says. “When you short-circuited Protobot, you deleted his mission to steal the island’s coins. You also freed me and the other agents. I’d say you’ve done really well, Rookie.”

Rookie beams. “Really, G? Thanks!”

“I’m sorry you didn’t impress Jet Pack Guy,” you say.

“Just wait!” Rookie says confidently. “Now that G says I did a good job, I feel like I can do anything!”

THE END

CONTINUED FROM PAGE 54.

"The hole is right here," you say. "Let's check it out."

"Sounds good to me!" Rookie says. "I'll go first!"

Rookie shimmies down the hole, and you follow him in. After you go a few feet, you drop down into what looks like some kind of tunnel. There's just enough sunlight coming through the hole that you can still see.

"What is this place?" you ask.

"I'm not sure," Rookie says. "Maybe it's where the real golden puffle lives! Wouldn't that be cool?"

"Let's look around," you say.

Rookie takes out a flashlight. "This should help."

You both slowly make your way down the tunnel, which leads to a door. You open it and enter a large room. Rookie's flashlight illuminates a big lever on one of the walls.

"Hmm," Rookie says, pulling the lever. "Maybe it leads to the entrance of the puffle lair."

Whoosh! Whoosh! Whoosh! A barrage of snowballs flies out of the wall, nearly hitting

you and Rookie! You both quickly dodge the snowballs and run farther into the room.

"Whoa!" you cry, steadying yourself. Something on the floor has tripped you up. You look down and see that you've stepped into a cardboard box.

"Rookie, wait up!" you yell. You kick off the box and catch up with your new friend.

Rookie is shining his flashlight into a corner of the room. Two glowing green eyes shine from the darkness.

"Wh-what's that?" you ask nervously.

"Don't move," Rookie whispers. He shines the flashlight from side to side—revealing a huge green crocodile!

"Scratch that," Rookie says. "Run!"

The two of you run as fast as you can in the opposite direction—and run smack into a wall. Rookie's flashlight illuminates two doors, one next to the other.

"What is this place?" you ask.

"I have a theory," Rookie says. "The snowball trap, the crocodile—it's just like the lost world in *Quest for the Golden Puffle*! I think we've stumbled into another dimension.

Part of the box dimension, maybe."

Your eyes get wide. "If that's true, then maybe the real golden puffle *does* live here."

Rookie nods. "It might be waiting for us behind one of these doors. But which one?"

If you open the door on the right, go to page 64.

If you open the door on the left, go to page 73.

CONTINUED FROM PAGE 10.

You and Rookie decide to go to the Stage and waddle to the Plaza. The name of the play on the marquee is *Ruby and the Ruby.*

When you enter, you see that the stage is decorated to look like an old black-and-white movie. Several penguins are milling around in vintage suits and gowns, and you guess that they're actors in the play. But one penguin looks out of place. She's a crisp-looking penguin with short blond hair and a denim jacket over a blue shirt. She smiles when she sees Rookie.

"Rookie, glad you're here," she says matter-of-factly.

"Um, thanks," Rookie says. Then he looks at you. "This is Dot, the stealth expert for the EPF."

"Wow, it's an honor to meet you," you say.

"Thanks!" she replies warmly, and then she's all business. "So, you got here fast, Rookie. I just called G a few seconds ago."

"No, I—" Rookie begins, but you nudge him.

"This might be your chance to do something impressive," you whisper, and Rookie nods.

"Yeah, right, G. So what have we got here?" Rookie asks.

"Well, like I told G, the ruby that's used in the play was stolen," she says, motioning for you to follow. She walks to an open safe that's part of the set of the play. "It used to be here, and now it's not. I was over at the Pizza Parlor when it was reported stolen, so G asked me to come over. But I'm happy to turn things over to you. I'm working on a real breakthrough in disguise back in the stealth lab, and I'd like to get back to it."

"Sure thing!" Rookie says confidently. "You can count on me, Dot!"

"I know I can," she replies. "Now don't forget to give G a report when you're done."

Dot rushes off, leaving you and Rookie to figure out the mystery of the missing ruby. Rookie eagerly rubs his flippers together.

"We've got a case to solve, and everyone's a suspect!" he says. He points at a red penguin in a blond wig, wearing a long dress. "You! What do you know about the ruby?"

"I don't know anything!" the actor protests, throwing her flippers in the air. "It was

missing when I got here."

You decide to leave the questioning to Rookie and start looking around the stage area. First, you examine the safe. It looks pretty clean. But when you look down, you notice something on the floor.

The stage floor is a bit dusty, and there are some strange tracks in the dust. You bend down to examine them. It looks like the tracks of something small, with four legs—no, claws. A crab?

Excited, you rush to tell Rookie what you've found. "Excuse me, Rookie, but I found some interesting tracks on the floor."

But Rookie is distracted. "The ruby isn't on the floor," he says absently. He begins to pace. "Someone in this room must know where the ruby is, and nobody is leaving until I find out!"

Then he stops. "Look! There are some interesting tracks on the floor!"

"That's what I was trying to tell you," you say. "I think they're crab tracks."

Rookie bends down. "You're right! Good work! Let's follow them."

The tracks lead to the back door and

then disappear, covered by some freshly fallen snow.

"We lost them!" you say.

"Not necessarily," Rookie says. "We know the thief is a crab. Now we just need to go to a place where crabs are found."

If you go to the Beach, go to page 33.

If you go to the Iceberg, go to page 55.

CONTINUED FROM PAGE 72.

You grab the cup of water and throw it at Protobot.

Splash! The water soaks the robot. He sizzles and sparks, and his arms begin to wildly spin around. Then the yellow glow in his eyes fades, and Protobot stops moving.

"Good job!" Rookie cheers. "You short-circuited Protobot!"

Bzzz. Whrrrrrr. Beeeeeep.

Strange sounds start coming from Protobot now. His yellow eyes blink back to life.

"System compromised," Protobot says. "Must reboot." Then he starts to roll away.

"Oh, man, that thing is unstoppable!" you wail.

Rookie jumps up and chases after Protobot, but the robot is surprisingly fast. He rolls away from the conference area toward the EPF mainframe.

You and Rookie chase him through the winding halls of HQ. By the time you catch up to him, Protobot has plugged into the mainframe.

"Oh no! He's infecting the system!" Rookie

cries. “We should go back and free Jet Pack Guy and the others. They’ll know what to do.”

Rookie starts to run, but you stop him.

“You wanted to impress Jet Pack Guy, right?” you ask. “Well, this is your chance. If we can bring up *System Defender*, we might be able to bring down Protobot for good.”

You’ve trained on *System Defender* before. It’s a complex system of cannons used to protect the EPF mainframe.

“You have a point,” Rookie says. “While Protobot is rebooting, he’s like a sitting duck. I’m just not sure if I have the skills to do it.”

If you decide to try to use *System Defender*, go to page 20.

If you decide to free the trapped agents, go to page 75.

CONTINUED FROM PAGE 35.

“Let’s go to the Night Club,” Rookie says. “There’s always music there.”

You waddle back into town and enter the Night Club. A loud bass beat is thumping from the big black speakers, and penguins are showing off their best moves. On a platform behind the dance floor, a purple penguin wearing a baseball cap is spinning tunes on the turntables.

Rookie starts spinning and grooving on the dance floor.

“Rookie,” you remind him, “we’re here to find Herbert.”

“Oh, sorry,” Rookie says. “Let’s look around.”

Everything seems normal in the Night Club. You don’t find any signs of Herbert.

“Let’s question the dancers,” Rookie suggests, when suddenly his spy phone rings.

Rookie looks at the screen. “We’ve got to go,” he tells you. “G has a new assignment for me.”

Go to page 79.

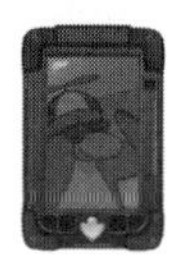

CONTINUED FROM PAGE 28.

"That catapult looks fun!" Rookie says. "Let's try it!"

You and Rookie transport back to the tree and set up the catapult.

"Um, do you want me to go up in that thing?" you ask a little bit nervously.

"Well, sure, if you want to," Rookie says. He sounds disappointed.

"No, no, that's okay," you assure him. "You get in the basket, and I'll work the lever."

Rookie eagerly hops in the basket. He firmly plants his propeller beanie on his head and adjusts his glasses.

"Ready!" he calls out.

You take a deep breath and grip the lever. "Okay, here goes. One . . . two . . . three!"

You pull the lever with all your might, releasing the catapult. The device flings Rookie, up, up, up into the air.

"Wheeeeeeeee!"

You watch, amazed, as Rookie grabs onto one of the top tree branches midflight.

"I think I see a puffle!" he calls down to you.

"Nice!" you reply. "But I just thought of something. How are you going to get down?"

"I'll climb!" Rookie calls back.

Then Rookie disappears from view, and all you can see is the rustling of tree branches up ahead. Then you see the branches move as Rookie climbs down.

"I can't go the rest of the way with just one flipper," he calls down to you. "Catch!"

Before you can protest, you see something yellow fall from the branches. You race underneath it and catch it. It's a yellow puffle!

Rookie jumps down next to you. "Isn't it a cute little guy? It must have looked golden when the sun hit it."

"Too bad we didn't find the real golden puffle," you say.

"Aw, that's no big deal. I'm just glad we saved this one!" Rookie answers. "Let's head to the Pet Shop. This guy needs some food and water."

You and Rookie head into the Plaza, carrying the puffle. As you approach the Stage, a crowd of excited penguins surrounds you.

"You found it!"

"Where did you find it?"

"We've been looking everywhere!"

"What is everyone talking about?" you wonder out loud.

A purple penguin waddles up and explains things. "Haven't you read the newspaper? The yellow puffle known as the Keeper of the Stage has been missing for days. But you found it!"

The happy yellow puffle hops out of Rookie's arms and hops onto the Stage. Everyone cheers.

"Looks like you're a hero, Rookie," you say.

"That makes you one, too!" Rookie says.

The next day, the rescue of the yellow puffle makes the front page of *The Club Penguin Times*. You're happy because for a little while, you're famous around Club Penguin. And Rookie is happy because Jet Pack Guy actually gives him a compliment.

"Nice work, Rookie."

THE END

CONTINUED FROM PAGE 69.

"Well, Ski Hill is closest," Rookie says. "Let's check that out first."

The Ski Village is nestled in the foothills of the mountains on Club Penguin. There, penguins can hang out in the cozy Ski Lodge, check out the Everyday Phoning Facility, or go sled racing down one of the fast-paced runs on the Ski Hill.

"I'm sure the dart on that Mullet fish was in the exact spot of the top of this hill," he says confidently. "I'm sure we'll find Herbert up here, carrying out his evil plans."

Your chair crests the top of the hill, and Rookie cries, "Look! It's him!"

He jumps off the chair in a flash, somersaulting onto the fluffy snow below. Just past him, you see a tall, white figure. Your heart races. Is it really Herbert?

But a split second later, you realize the truth—it's just a penguin in a puffy white suit. Before you can stop Rookie, he's tackling the penguin.

"Gotcha!" Rookie cries triumphantly.

“Rookie, get off me!” barks a deep voice. The penguin pulls down his hood. It’s Jet Pack Guy!

“Uh-oh,” you whisper.

“Sorry, Jet Pack Guy,” Rookie says. “I thought you were Herbert.”

“Do I look like a polar bear?” Jet Pack Guy asks. “I’m testing out a new field suit for G.”

“My bad,” Rookie says sheepishly.

Jet Pack Guy sighs. “Let’s go back to HQ.”

The three of you transport to EPF Headquarters, where G is pleased to see you. The blue penguin is known as Gary the Gadget Guy outside the EPF.

“Excellent test, Agents,” G says. “That suit took a beating from you, Rookie, and I got some useful readings.”

“You mean it was good that I tackled Jet Pack Guy?” Rookie asks.

G nods. “Definitely.”

Jet Pack Guy shakes his head. “Not bad, Rookie!”

THE END

CONTINUED FROM PAGE 10.

"My intuition is telling me that the red penguin's friend's brother's cousin really did see the golden puffle," Rookie says. "To the Forest!"

"Why not?" you say, and you and your new friend waddle away from the Town Center toward the Forest.

When you leave the Plaza and step onto the snowy Forest path, you're struck by how peaceful things suddenly feel. The majestic pine trees surrounding you keep out the noisy sounds from the busy parts of Club Penguin.

Not that the Forest is deserted. Several penguins are waddling around, making new friends and talking about their favorite spots and games on the island.

"We need to interview everyone here," Rookie says, sounding snappy and professional.

"I'll stick with you," you say. You're a little bit nervous about investigating on your own, and Rookie seems to know what he's doing.

Rookie approaches two penguins who are talking under a pine tree.

"Excuse me," he says. "Has either of you seen a golden puffle?"

"Sure, it's one of my favorite plays," replies one of them, a pink penguin.

"No, we mean a *real* golden puffle," you clarify.

The pink penguin shakes her head. "No, but I heard that guy talking about one." She points to a green penguin.

"Sure, I saw it," says the green penguin after Rookie asks him. "It was flying! I saw it fly over those trees over there." He points to a spot in the distance.

"Wow, that's great!" Rookie says excitedly, but then a red penguin approaches.

"I saw the golden puffle, too," he says. "But it wasn't flying. It hopped down into a hole."

If you head for the trees, go to page 25.

If you climb down into the hole, go to page 38.

CONTINUED FROM PAGE 44.

"The last time I used the Aqua Grabber at the Iceberg, I saw a crab in the ocean," you say. "I think his name is Klepto."

"I think you're onto something," Rookie says. "Klepto is a notorious thief. He's always trying to steal the Puffle O's in the *Puffle Launch* game. Let's head to the Iceberg!"

You and Rookie take out your spy phones and use them to instantly transport to the Iceberg. As usual, it's crowded with penguins in hard hats using jackhammers to drill into the ice. They're trying to get the Iceberg to tip over, but as far as you know, that's never really happened. But penguins keep trying.

"To the Aqua Grabber!" Rookie says. Invented by Gary the Gadget Guy, penguins use this minisubmarine to explore the ocean depths, looking for treasure. It's a round craft with a clear, bubble-shaped dome over the cockpit, making it look like some kind of UFO.

Once you and Rookie are inside, Rookie works the controls to lower the craft below the ocean's surface. The blue water becomes darker,

the deeper you descend. Down below, you see brightly colored plants growing on the ocean floor. Orange starfish skitter among them.

"It's beautiful down here," you say.

"It'll be more beautiful if we can find that ruby," Rookie says. "Keep your eyes open for anything suspicious."

Rookie steers the Aqua Grabber back and forth. Huge air bubbles rise up from vents in the ground, and Rookie steers right into one.

"We've got to make sure we don't run out of air," Rookie warns.

"Hey, is that a cave?" you ask, pointing to a dark spot past a strand of twisting coral.

"I think so," Rookie says. "Let's check it out."

He steers inside the pitch-black cave. The Aqua Grabber's headlights illuminate the space, making you and Rookie gasp.

The cave is littered with stuff from all over Club Penguin. There are coffee cups from the Coffee Shop, empty pizza trays from the Pizza Parlor, colorful seashells, and on top of the pile is one glittering, shining red ruby.

"The stolen ruby!" you cry.

"Looks like we've caught that criminal crab in the act," Rookie says. "Let's retrieve the stolen property."

He pulls a lever on the control panel, and a metal arm with a claw descends from the bottom of the Aqua Grabber. Carefully steering, he grips the ruby with the claw.

"Let's get out of here," Rookie says.

Suddenly, an angry red crab appears in the window in front of you.

"It's Klepto!" you shout.

"He's making a big mistake if he thinks he can get this ruby back from Rookie," your new friend says. "Hang on!"

Rookie presses a button, and the Aqua Grabber shoots forward at an amazing speed. You glance behind you and see that Klepto is right on your tail.

"Faster, Rookie!" you urge.

Rookie steers the Aqua Grabber across the ocean floor, dodging rocks, coral, and plants. Then he frowns.

"We're running out of air!" he cries.

You quickly scan the scene.

"There's an air vent over by that rock to

your left," you say. "Otherwise, I think I see one up ahead."

**If you try the vent up ahead,
go to page 11.**

**If you try the vent near the rock,
go to page 23.**

CONTINUED FROM PAGE 77.

Protobot rolls past your hiding place.

"Rookie, do something!" you urge.

Rookie takes out a small blue pouch. "Okay, trusty marble collection. Let's see what you can do."

He empties the pouch, spilling marbles right across Protobot's path. The marbles mess up Protobot's wheels, and the big robot crashes to the floor.

"Awesome!" Rookie cheers, giving you a high five.

"Protobot doesn't stay down for long," you remind him. "Is there any way to shut him down before he can get back up?"

"I'm on it!" Rookie says, jumping up. He bravely climbs onto Protobot's back. The robot is facedown on the floor. His wheels are spinning and his arms are flailing as he tries to get up.

"You cannot defeat me," Protobot says, but from that position he doesn't seem so scary anymore.

"What do you know? An off switch!" Rookie cries. He presses a button, and the yellow glow

fades from Protobot's eyes.

The sound of cannon fire stops, and Jet Pack Guy, Dot, and G rush up to you.

"Stand back!" Jet Pack Guy says. "I'll handle this!"

"Already did!" Rookie says cheerfully, jumping off Protobot's back. "This bucket of bolts won't be going anywhere."

G examines Protobot. "Excellent work, Rookie," he says, and he nods to you. "And you, too."

"It was all Rookie," you say. "He's a pretty amazing agent."

Jet Pack Guy nods. "Nice job," he says. "Maybe you and I can work on a case together sometime."

"Me? You want me?" Rookie asks. He turns to you. "Whoopee! Did you hear that? Jet Pack Guy wants to work with *this* guy. This guy right here!"

He's proudly pointing to himself, and you smile. You wanted to help Rookie impress Jet Pack Guy. Looks like you've accomplished your mission!

THE END

CONTINUED FROM PAGE 69.

"Hmm," Rookie says thoughtfully. "The Lighthouse is by the water. The Cove is by the water. So let's try the Cove first."

"Sounds good to me," you agree.

You follow Rookie out of the Lighthouse and across the island to the Cove. This out-of-the-way location is a favorite place for penguins to swim and surf. Roaring flames leap up from the fire pit, and some penguins are hanging out at the Surf Hut. A yellow penguin sits in the lifeguard chair, looking through binoculars at penguins splashing in the water.

"Looks pretty normal to me," you say.

"That's why we need to look closer," Rookie says. "I need to comb every inch of the Cove until I find a clue."

You sigh. Rookie is very dedicated, but you're pretty sure he's wasting time. Still, he's a lot of fun to be around, so you decide to help him.

"I'll check out the Surf Hut," you offer.

"Thanks!" Rookie says. "I'll start with the lifeguard chair."

You waddle over to the Surf Hut, admiring the colorful surfboards on display outside. You're not exactly sure what you're looking for, but you look around, anyway.

Then you see it—behind the Surf Hut is an open can of something sticky. You lean down to get a closer look.

"Pizza grease?" you ask. "What is that doing here?"

You call Rookie over. "Rookie, you'd better come see this!"

Rookie quickly joins you and frowns when he sees the pizza grease. "Very suspicious. Let's see what else we can find."

Rookie starts to look around and quickly spots something you didn't see because it's white and sitting on top of the snow.

"Check it out," Rookie says excitedly. "Polar bear fur! Herbert must have been here!"

You're pretty impressed—it looks like Rookie was onto something after all. He takes out his spy phone and calls G.

"G, I found some of Herbert's fur by the Surf Hut," he says. "Along with a can of pizza grease."

You can hear G's reply through the speaker. "Aha! That explains this mysterious message I received. It says, 'I hate seeing penguins having so much fun playing *Catchin' Waves*. Now they'll be catching nothing but trouble!' Herbert must be trying to sabotage the surfing game."

"I bet he polished the surfboards with pizza grease!" Rookie says. "That'll be sure to send penguins sliding off their surfboards!"

"Don't let anyone near the surfboards," G says. "I'll send some backup."

A few minutes later, Jet Pack Guy zips into the Cove.

"G tells me you cracked the surfboard case," he says. "Nice work, Rookie."

Rookie lights up. "Gee, thanks, Jet Pack Guy! So are you saying that you're . . . impressed?"

"Sure," Jet Pack Guy says.

"Woo-hoo!" cheers Rookie, and you give him a high five.

"I knew you could do it!" you tell him.

THE END

CONTINUED FROM PAGE 40.

You slowly open the door on the right. To your surprise, you see that you and Rookie are backstage at the Stage!

"I have a feeling we weren't in another dimension," you say.

Rookie looks sad. "We were so close to the golden puffle! I'll never impress Jet Pack Guy now."

"Did somebody say Jet Pack Guy?"

The sunglass-wearing EPF Agent walks up between you and Rookie, surprising you.

"Jet Pack Guy! What are you doing here?" Rookie asked.

"G asked me to investigate a mystery," he replies. "Want to partner with me on this one?"

"Do I? You bet I do!" Rookie says happily. He turns to you and shakes your flipper. "Thanks for your help, but I've got to get busy on this case with *Jet Pack Guy*!"

You can see that your new friend is thrilled, and that makes you happy. Maybe one day, you think, you'll be able to investigate with him again.

THE END

CONTINUED FROM PAGE 74.

Rookie skids to a stop.

"Thanks for the warning," he says. "I'll jump over it."

Rookie hops over the top step and climbs the platform until he reaches the golden puffle. He triumphantly picks it up.

"Ta-da!" he announces. And then he falls.

"Wait a minute, this isn't a real puffle," he says.

"What do you mean?" you ask.

Rookie climbs back down and hands the golden puffle to you. It's not too heavy, and it's definitely not fuzzy.

"I think it's wrapped in golden foil," you say. You peel off a little bit, see something dark underneath, and sniff it. "Mmm, chocolate!"

"Just like in the play," Rookie says. "I'm starting to think we're not in an alternate dimension."

You're thinking the same thing. You point to a door next to the platform. "I think we'll find our answers there."

You and Rookie step through the door—and find yourselves backstage at the Stage! A navy-

blue penguin wearing a director's cap rushes up to you.

"Awesome!" he exclaims. "That door to the prop room has been stuck for days. We've been trying to get in there so we can put up the set for our next play. Thanks to you, the show will go on!"

Rookie smiles. "Just doing our job, friend. Just doing our job!"

The director of the play hurries off to spread the good news.

"Sorry we didn't find the real golden puffle," you say. "I know you wanted to impress Jet Pack Guy."

"Hey, we saved the play, and that's a big deal," Rookie says. "I can always impress Jet Pack Guy tomorrow!"

THE END

CONTINUED FROM PAGE 35.

"The Lighthouse sounds good!" Rookie says. "Let's go!"

You and Rookie waddle over to the Lighthouse. Inside, it looks like you've stumbled onto some kind of party. Some penguins are seated in the folding chairs, chatting. Others are on the stage, tuning their instruments and warming up. Other penguins are putting up colorful decorations.

"Looks like a simple party," you remark.

"To the untrained eye," Rookie says, getting into detective mode. "But I view everything through the eyes of a trained EPF Agent."

Rookie strolls over to a red balloon. "This may look like an ordinary balloon to you. But it's the perfect vehicle for a secret message!"

Rookie produces a sewing needle.

Pop! The balloon pops loudly, and everyone in the room jumps. The deflated balloon sinks to the floor, with no secret message inside.

"Okay, so maybe there's no message in this one," Rookie says. "We'll just have to check all of them."

You gently lead Rookie away. "There must be some other clues around here," you say.

"Of course!" Rookie says. He jumps up on stage and tears down a long blue streamer. "These might look like ordinary streamers, but I bet they contain a secret code."

Rookie examines the streamer and frowns. "Hmm. This one is blank. Herbert must have used invisible ink."

"Or maybe it's just a decoration," you say. "I think that message you found was just a flyer for the party."

Rookie is concentrating so hard that he doesn't hear you. He strolls up to the wall, where some penguins have started a game of Pin the Tail on the Mullet. There's a picture of a Mullet, a large red fish, on the wall, and there are two darts stuck in it.

"Excuse me," he says to the two penguins, who step aside. Rookie nods at you. "This may look like an ordinary game. But see how this fish is shaped like Club Penguin? I think these darts represent where Herbert will strike."

"What do you mean?" you ask.

Rookie points to a dart. "See this one here,

near the tail? On a map of Club Penguin, this would be the Cove. And this other dart, over by the eye, would be Ski Hill."

You think Rookie is imagining things, but getting him out of the Lighthouse now seems like a good idea.

"Okay," you say. "So where should we go?"

If you go to Ski Hill, go to page 51.
If you go to the Cove, go to page 61.

CONTINUED FROM PAGE 80.

"Pizza is great, but coins are everywhere," you point out. "You earn them when you do jobs or play games. You can use them to buy cool things. And when penguins donate coins to the Coins For Change program, they help people, animals, and environments all over the world."

"I can't argue with that," Rookie says. "So, if Protobot is going after the coins, we should probably tell G!"

You and Rookie hurry to the Everyday Phoning Facility in the Ski Village. When you enter, the innocent-looking pay telephone turns into a screen that reads, "WELCOME, AGENTS." A column in the corner rises to reveal the tube transport that leads to HQ.

Whoosh! The tube quickly takes you down, down . . . and then opens up on an incredible scene. Dot, Jet Pack Guy, and G (the EPF Agent and inventor also known as Gary the Gadget Guy) are inside a cage that's crackling and sparkling with electricity. Looming over them is a big robot with yellow, glowing eyes. His body is made up of items from around Club Penguin,

including a mine cart and a ticket booth.

"Protobot!" Rookie yells.

The robot turns his head. "I am Protobot. Surrender, intruder."

Rookie looks angry. "I will *not* surrender! You're messing with Rookie now!"

Rookie charges at Protobot, hoping to reach his control panel and shut him down. But as he races up the steps, he trips and comes tumbling back down. He rolls under a conference table, and you race to his side.

"I am Protobot. Resistance is pointless."

The robot moves toward you both now. Rookie groans and sits up while you look around for something—anything—that you can use to defend yourself.

"Be careful!" Dot calls from the cage. "Protobot was looking for Club Penguin's coins but couldn't find them. He trapped us so that he can hook into the EPF mainframe and find their location. There's no stopping him."

Protobot is getting closer every second. The only thing within reach is what looks like the remains of an Agent's lunch—a cup of water from the watercooler and an apple. It's

all you've got to work with, and Protobot is advancing fast.

If you toss the apple at Protobot, go to page 29.

If you throw the cup of water at Protobot, go to page 45.

CONTINUED FROM PAGE 40.

"Let's try the door on the left," you say.

Rookie slowly opens the door and steps inside. You follow behind him. Almost immediately, you hear a loud thump.

"Uh-oh!" Rookie cries, and he drops his flashlight. The room goes dark.

"Rookie, what happened?" you ask.

"I tripped over something," he says.

"Hold on," you tell him. "I'm coming."

You hurry forward—and *bam!* You trip, too. Rookie must have knocked over a box of long, white bandages, because they're all over you. You try to get back on your feet, but you get tangled in the bandages.

"Found the flashlight!" Rookie calls out.

"Oh good," you say, finally standing up. "I need some help with my—"

"MUMMY!" Rookie yells. He's staring at you and pointing.

"Stand back, Mummy," he says. "Your ancient Egyptian powers can't hurt me."

You take a step forward to explain when one of the bandages wraps around your beak.

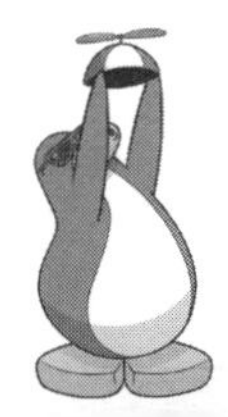

"I'm warning you, Mummy," Rookie says. "I'm a secret agent."

You pull the bandages off your beak. "Rookie, it's me! I got wrapped up in those bandages you knocked over."

Rookie relaxes. "Wow, you scared me! I thought this other dimension was full of mummies."

Rookie unwraps your bandages, and the two of you continue your exploration. Moving forward, Rookie's flashlight illuminates a tall, stacked platform. There's something shining on the very top.

"It's the golden puffle!" Rookie yells. As he races toward the platform, you notice that the first step looks suspicious.

"Hey, Rookie, watch out for that first step!" you yell.

If Rookie climbs the platform, go to page 65.

If Rookie steps on the first step of the platform, go to page 78.

CONTINUED FROM PAGE 46.

"Let's not chance it," you say. "Come on, let's go free those guys!"

You race back to the main room, and G instructs Rookie to pull a lever on the wall. It cancels the electric charge in the cage, and Jet Pack Guy opens the lock, freeing himself, Dot, and G.

"Where's Protobot?" Jet Pack Guy asks.

"He's infected the EPF mainframe," Rookie reports. "But we think we can use *System Defender* to take him down."

"I'm on it!" Jet Pack Guy says, quickly dashing away.

"Dot and I will accompany Jet Pack Guy," G tells you and Rookie. He's a blue penguin wearing round eyeglasses and a white lab coat. "Rookie, you stay here and make sure no other Agents enter. It's too dangerous."

"But, G, I want to be where the action is!" Rookie protests.

"This is an important job, too, Rookie," G says. Then he and Dot take off after Jet Pack Guy.

Rookie sighs. "I never get to do anything cool."

"Well, at least we can watch it," you say, turning on a screen attached to the surveillance system. "Look!"

You see that Jet Pack Guy is trying to call up *System Defender*.

"It's not working!" he says. "Whatever Protobot is doing to the mainframe seems to have crashed it."

G steps in front of him. "Let me try."

He starts typing quickly on the keyboard. "You're correct. But I am able to bring up a few red cannons."

"Better than nothing," Dot says, and she activates them.

Bam! Bam! Bam! The cannons shoot at Protobot but miss. The robot spins around, his eyes blazing.

"I cannot be destroyed," he says. "Reboot ninety-nine percent complete."

Protobot's eyes flash on and off, and the red cannons spin around. Now they're aimed at the EPF Agents.

"Everybody duck!" Jet Pack Guy yells.

Even though you and Rookie are in the next

room, you both dive under a table—those cannons are serious. On the screen, you see Protobot rolling away from the mainframe. The robot is headed back to the Control Room!

"We can't let him escape!" you yell.

"I know," Rookie says. "We've got to think. I don't have any weapons on me—just my lucky marble collection. I never go anywhere without it."

From your position under the table, you see a panel of flashing lights marked CONTROL ROOM.

"What does that thing do?" you ask Rookie.

"I'm not sure," he replies, "but I think maybe it secures the Control Room."

If Rookie presses a button on the control panel, go to page 36.

If Rookie uses his marble collection to stop Protobot, go to page 59.

CONTINUED FROM PAGE 74.

Rookie is in such a hurry to grab the golden puffle that he ignores you. When he reaches the platform, he steps right on the first step.

The wall behind the platform opens up, and a huge boulder rolls out!

“Run!” you yell.

You and Rookie race across the room. You reach a door marked EMERGENCY EXIT. You push as hard as you can, and you and Rookie emerge into the bright sunshine.

“Rats!” Rookie exclaims. “The golden puffle is still in there. We’ve got to get back into that dimension.”

“Um, I’m starting to think that wasn’t another dimension,” you say, looking around. “It kind of looks like we’re behind the Stage.”

But Rookie is so excited that he doesn’t hear you.

“No matter how long it takes, no matter what I have to do, I will impress Jet Pack Guy!” he vows.

THE END

CONTINUED FROM PAGE 47.

"What's the assignment?" you ask.

Rookie reads the message on his phone. "'I have intercepted a strange message at the Recycling Plant, and I need you to decode it.'"

"A message?" you ask. "Do you think it's from Herbert?"

"Could be," Rookie says. "Come on, let's go."

The Recycling Plant is a green glass building next to the entrance of the Mine. Rookie heads right for the large control panel that runs the recycling machine and turns on the screen.

"Here's the message. It looks like a typical substitution cipher," he explains, "where each shape stands for a letter of the alphabet."

He types on the keyboard for a bit, concentrating. After a few minutes, he stops.

"Got it!" he exclaims. "It says, 'I am Protobot. You thought I was destroyed, but you are incorrect. I have returned to destroy Club Penguin's most precious resource. Surrender now. You cannot stop me.'"

"Whoa," you say. "You got all that from

a bunch of shapes? Cool! And who's Protobot, anyway? Another villain?"

Rookie nods. "It all started when G built these three Test Bots to help with his experiments. But they went haywire and built Protobot out of stuff on the island. Protobot turned out bigger and stronger than the Test Bots. The EPF destroyed him, but Herbert rebuilt him. Then the EPF destroyed him *again*, but it looks like he's back."

"And now he's after Club Penguin's most precious resource," you say. "What do you think that is?"

"Pizza!" Rookie exclaims. "Everyone loves pizza!"

"True," you agree. "But is it really precious? What about coins?"

If you and Rookie go to the Pizza Parlor, go to page 13.

If you try to convince Rookie that coins are more valuable than pizza, go to page 70.